Dear Parent:
Your child's love of reading starts here!

Every child learns to read in a different way and at his or her own speed. Some go back and forth between reading levels and read favorite books again and again. Others read through each level in order. You can help your young reader improve and become more confident by encouraging his or her own interests and abilities. From books your child reads with you to the first books he or she reads alone, there are I Can Read Books for every stage of reading:

SHARED READING
Basic language, word repetition, and whimsical illustrations, ideal for sharing with your emergent reader

BEGINNING READING
Short sentences, familiar words, and simple concepts for children eager to read on their own

READING WITH HELP
Engaging stories, longer sentences, and language play for developing readers

READING ALONE
Complex plots, challenging vocabulary, and high-interest topics for the independent reader

ADVANCED READING
Short paragraphs, chapters, and exciting themes for the perfect bridge to chapter books

I Can Read Books have introduced children to the joy of reading since 1957. Featuring award-winning authors and illustrators and a fabulous cast of beloved characters, I Can Read Books set the standard for beginning readers.

A lifetime of discovery begins with the magical words **"I Can Read!"**

Visit www.icanread.com for information
on enriching your child's reading experience.

Library of Congress catalog card number: 2012942502
ISBN 978-0-06-207487-4 (trade bdg.)—ISBN 978-0-06-207486-7 (pbk.)

13 14 15 16 SCP 10 9 8 7 6 5 4 3 2 1   ❖   First Edition

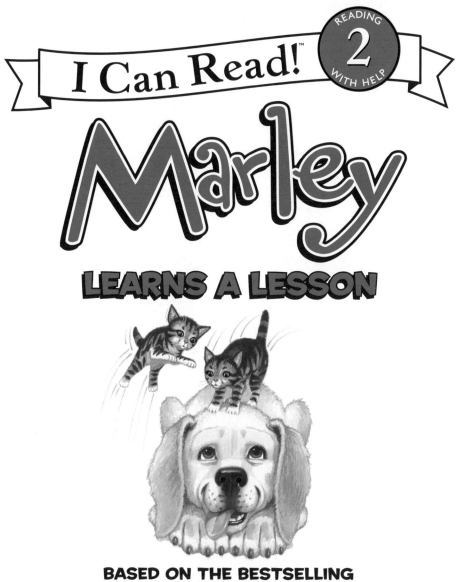

I Can Read!

READING 2 WITH HELP

Marley

LEARNS A LESSON

**BASED ON THE BESTSELLING
BOOKS BY JOHN GROGAN**

COVER ART BY RICHARD COWDREY

TEXT BY CAITLIN BIRCH

INTERIOR ILLUSTRATIONS BY RICK WHIPPLE

HARPER
An Imprint of HarperCollinsPublishers

Cassie's family had two new kittens.
Their names were Lucky and Yow-Yow.

Marley loved Lucky and Yow-Yow.
He wanted to teach them
all of life's important things.

7

Marley showed Lucky and Yow-Yow
that the kittens in the mirror
are not real kittens.

Marley taught the kittens to wait
by the door for Cassie
to come home from school.

Marley taught the kittens

not to get too close

to Baby Louie's diaper.

"Danger!" warned Marley.

Lucky and Yow-Yow wanted
to teach Marley
some new things, too.
The kittens taught Marley
how to pounce.

15

The kittens taught Marley
their favorite game.

17

The kittens taught Marley

how to sharpen his claws.

"No, Marley, no!" Mommy yelled.

"Go to your doghouse, Marley.
We are going out for a little bit."
But Mommy didn't say that Marley
had to go to the doghouse
all by himself.

Marley led Lucky and Yow-Yow out
to his doghouse.

At first it was fun outside,

but then Marley heard a low rumble.

A storm was coming.

Marley did not like storms.

Soon, thunder rolled.

Lightning flashed.

Marley was scared.

Marley ran back inside.

Howwwwwwl!

Marley showed the kittens
how to howl at something scary.

The kittens didn't howl.

The kittens didn't cry.

They curled up with Marley.

Marley felt their soft fur.

He heard their gentle purring.

Boooom went the thunder.

Crack went the lightning.

And then, as quickly as it
had come,
the storm was gone.
All was well again.

Marley felt better.

"Maybe storms aren't so scary
after all," Marley thought.
He felt so much better
that he fell asleep.

29

When Marley woke up,
the family was home.
"Marley and the kittens
weathered the storm just fine,"
Daddy said.

Yow-Yow yawned and stretched.

Lucky licked Marley's paw.

Marley felt so happy,
he wished he could learn
how to purr.